Little Passports®
A GLOBAL ADVENTURE

A Recipe for Adventure

Written by Megan E. Bryant

Illustrated by Carrie English

Sam & Sofia's Scooter Stories

First paperback edition printed in 2019 by Little Passports, Inc.
Copyright © 2019 Little Passports
All rights reserved
Select quotations included from *The Wonderful Wizard of Oz* by L. Frank Baum
Book design by Carly Queen
Manufactured in China
10 9 8 7 6

Little Passports, Inc.
27 Maiden Lane, Suite 400, San Francisco, CA 94108
www.littlepassports.com
ISBN: 978-1-953148-00-1

Contents

1 Compass Community Center 1
2 Aunt Charlie's Invention 11
3 Whiz … Zoom … FOOP! 23
4 The Scooter Secret 30
5 The Hiding Place 40
6 An Unexpected Breeze 44
7 Special Delivery 50
8 The Chase 54
9 Out of Town 62
10 An Unbelievable Beach 66
11 The Amazing Amazon 77
12 One Last Stop 90
13 No Place Like Home 93

1
Compass Community Center

"**P**apai?" Sofia called. She skipped down the long hallway of Compass Community Center, peeking into each room she passed. She knew her father, Luiz, was here somewhere, but where? Not in the music room, where musicians jammed on the drums. Not in the kitchen, where Mama was busy preparing for the Seventh Annual Compass Community Center Potluck Dinner. Not in the art studio, where some of Papai's students were painting signs for the potluck. Not in the gym, not in the game room, not in the library. Even Papai's office was empty.

Or was it?

"Papai?" Sofia called again, staring curiously at the ladder in the middle of the room. It stood beneath a gaping hole in the ceiling.

"Sofia?" Papai's voice replied. Sofia could definitely *hear* her dad, but she couldn't see him.

"Where are you?" Sofia asked.

Papai poked his head down through the opening in the ceiling. "*Olá, minha filha!*" he said.

"Papai!" Sofia giggled. "What are you doing up there?"

Sofia ran over to hold the ladder steady as Papai climbed down.

"I've been searching high and low—no exaggeration!—for my old scrapbook. I can't find it anywhere," Papai said, brushing dust off his pants.

"I didn't know you had a scrapbook," Sofia said.

"Yes, yes. I made it when I was a boy," Papai told her.

Sofia's dark brown eyes brightened. She loved to hear stories about Papai's childhood in

Brazil, where his whole family lived in the same apartment building in São Paulo.

"Everything special to me, everything that mattered most, I put in that book," Papai said. "Photos and clippings... cards and letters... special notes and reminders I wrote for myself. I was getting ready for the potluck when I remembered it. I haven't thought about it in years."

"Oh, no! Is it lost?" Sofia asked.

"No, no, not lost," Papai said. "I put it somewhere very safe. Maybe too safe... because now even I can't remember where it is."

"Do you want to bring it to the potluck?" Sofia asked.

"Even better—I want to make my favorite dessert from when I was a boy and share it with everyone tonight," Papai said. He closed his eyes and licked his lips, as if he could taste it. "*Mousse de maracujá*. Passion fruit mousse! It was my *avó's* recipe, and I was the only one she

trusted with it."

Sofia grinned. Papai's stories about his feisty grandmother were legendary.

"So, naturally, I tucked it into my scrapbook and hid it away. Now I just have to remember where it is . . . " Papai said.

"Let's look together," Sofia suggested.

"Thank you," Papai said. "I bet your eagle eyes can spot all sorts of things I might have missed. Unless I left it back in my childhood apartment in São Paulo." Papai's usually cheerful face clouded over at the thought. "Well, hopefully not. If I did, I won't be able to make *mousse de maracujá* for the potluck."

Sofia's forehead wrinkled in confusion. "But Papai," she said, "couldn't you just call Tia Beatriz and ask her to read you the recipe over the phone?"

Papai chuckled. "Ahhh, but remember, even if the scrapbook is back in Brazil, I still don't know *where* in the apartment it might be," he said. "I had plenty of excellent hiding places when I was a boy. Some I remember and some I don't."

Just then, Sofia heard a distinct sound coming down the hallway. It was a cross between a **clink** and a **thwap**. She and her father exchanged a grin. There was only one person in all of Compass Court whose walk sounded like that: Sofia's best friend, Sam. It was the sound of one of his cameras bouncing on its strap around

his neck. And it was bouncing loud and fast! Sam must have been in a hurry, and he only hurried when he had news to share.

Sofia ducked into the hallway as Sam reached Papai's office. "Hey, Sam," she said with a wave. "What's up?"

"Sofia! You won't believe—" Sam began. His words tumbled out of his mouth in a rush. "Aunt Charlie's new invention—almost done—she just needs—"

"A tool?" Sofia guessed.

"Yes!" Sam said.

Sam's Aunt Charlie was a scientist and was always working on a new project. This one must have been really special to get Sam so excited.

"Can you come over to see it?" Sam asked. "It's a . . . well, actually, you'll just have to see for yourself!"

Sofia turned to Papai, who stood in the

doorway. "Of course you can go," he said, his eyes twinkling.

"Thanks, Papai Luiz," Sam said.

"Just be back in time for tonight's potluck," a voice said from behind them.

Sofia turned to see her mom, Lyla, pushing a cart full of food and kitchen utensils down the hall.

"Of course, Mama," Sofia said.

"We never miss a chance to help out in the kitchen, Mama Lyla," said Sam.

"I need my two favorite taste testers to make sure everything's perfect," Mama said.

Sofia's mother ran the community center. She knew everyone in Compass Court personally, and throwing community events was one of her favorite things to do.

"Things coming along nicely?" Papai asked her.

Mama smiled her warm smile. "Oh yes," Mama said. "These are the last of the ingredients. You kids have fun." Mama turned to Sam. "Tell your Aunt Charlie hello and we'll see her tonight."

Sofia hesitated. "What about your scrapbook?" she asked Papai.

Papai waved her worries away. "I'm sure it'll turn up," he said. "And if not, we'll look for it when you get back. Now go!"

2
Aunt Charlie's Invention

Sofia and Sam ran down the hall, pausing only to grab a wrench from the community center science room. Then they burst through the main doors of the community center and into the neighborhood, which buzzed with activity. But not even the ice cream truck at the curb or the dance-off in the courtyard could distract them today.

Sam and Aunt Charlie lived a block from the community center, across the street from Sofia's house. Sofia spent as much time at Sam's house as she did at her own. She especially loved to explore Aunt Charlie's lab in the garage. It was filled with high-tech gadgets and half-finished inventions. Best of all, Aunt Charlie always encouraged Sofia and Sam to build their own creations.

The friends went straight to the garage. "I can't wait to find out what it is," Sofia said. "Can't you give me a hint? Or a clue?"

Sam smiled and shook his head mysteriously. "Trust me. This surprise is worth the wait." He rapped on the garage door and opened it just a crack. "Aunt Charlie?"

"Come in, come in!" Aunt Charlie said. "I

don't know how I got this far without my two best assistants." She smiled at them from behind a pair of thick safety goggles that magnified her blue eyes, making them look wide and round.

Sofia reached into her pocket and pulled out a handful of tiny treasures, including two acorns, a chain of paperclips, a spare button, an itty-bitty notebook filled with to-do lists, and a small tin with six jelly beans in it. She sorted through the items until she found what she was looking for: a small piece of string. Sofia tied the string in a loop and pulled her hair into a ponytail. She did this whenever she was in the lab. If there was an experiment to do or a machine to build, she wanted to be ready to jump in and help.

"Here's your wrench," Sam said, handing his aunt the tool. "Sofia can't wait to find out what you've been up to."

"*Someone* wouldn't tell me anything," Sofia said. Then she turned to Aunt Charlie. "I heard you've been extra busy," she said, raising her eyebrows.

"You could say that," Aunt Charlie said. "You know how I get when something is just about done."

"Did you even go to bed last night?" Sam asked. "I heard you out here tinkering before the sun was up!"

"I might've been up a bit late," Aunt Charlie said. "But if you were me, wouldn't you have done the same thing? Allow me to present . . ."

With a **whoosh** and a **swoosh**, Aunt Charlie pulled a tarp off an oddly-shaped object in the corner.

Sofia sucked in her breath as her eyes grew wide. All she could say was "Wow!"

"Told you," Sam said with a grin.

Aunt Charlie's latest invention was like nothing she'd ever built before. She usually studied organisms under a microscope, combined different chemicals, or tinkered with small machines; she didn't usually work on vehicles. But here it was: a shiny red scooter, the color of candy apples.

"Voilà—my latest creation!" Aunt Charlie announced. "This isn't just a scooter. It's the smartest form of transportation anywhere in the world." She crouched down with the wrench and fiddled with some nuts and bolts on the underside of the scooter. "Just one last safety check to make sure everything's nice and tight," she said, "and there we go! It's done."

Aunt Charlie stepped back to let Sofia and Sam get a closer look. There was a seat for

the driver with a secret compartment hidden beneath, two handles, and—

"Is that a touch screen?" Sofia asked, staring at the glossy control panel.

"Yes, it is. This beauty is computerized. Well, sort of. It's actually a bit more complicated than that. You see, when you—"

Bzzzt! Bzzzt! Bzzzt!

Aunt Charlie glanced at her buzzing phone. A small frown flickered across her face. "Oh dear," she said. "Sofia, your mom says that one of the ovens isn't heating properly."

"Can you fix it?" Sam asked.

"I can certainly try," Aunt Charlie said. She grabbed her toolbox and stepped toward the door. "Feel free to check out the scooter. Just remember," she added with a wink, "there's no place like home." Then she ducked out of the garage, leaving them in the lab.

"I wonder what she meant by that," Sam said.

Sofia climbed onto the scooter's seat and glanced over at Sam. "Do you think she'll mind if we . . ."

"Of course not!" Sam said. "She just said we could check it out."

Sofia stared down at the screen. "Is this thing on?" she asked, touching it with her finger. Instantly, the screen began to glow. A globe appeared on the screen and began to slowly rotate. Sofia used her fingers to enlarge the image and realized—

"It's a map," she said. "A super-detailed map of . . . everywhere."

"Everywhere?" Sam asked, climbing onto the scooter behind her.

"Everywhere," she said. "The whole wide world."

Suddenly, yellow letters flashed across the screen.

"Good question," Sofia said, grinning. Her fingers skittered across the screen as she typed the first place that came to her mind.

The globe zoomed in on the country of Brazil. A pulsing dot appeared over the city of São Paulo.

A large green button appeared on the touch screen. The way it glowed captured Sofia's attention. Her finger hovered over the button. Should she . . . or shouldn't she . . . ?

Why not? Sofia thought.

"*Vamos,*" she whispered as she tapped the button.

It happened so fast, all Sofia and Sam could do was hold on tight. The touch screen, along with the scooter's headlamps and taillights, glowed so intensely that they formed a glittering globe of light around the scooter. Sofia stared, awestruck, at the shimmering orb that surrounded them until it became so bright she had to close her eyes against the blinding light.

Whiz . . . Zoom . . . FOOP!

3
Whiz ... Zoom ... FOOP!

Sofia opened her eyes, blinking over and over again as she looked around.

"Whoa," she breathed. "This is *definitely* not Aunt Charlie's lab."

"Sofia," Sam said. "Where *are* we?

What happened?"

"Sam, I don't think we're in Compass Court anymore," Sofia said. Gone were the familiar houses and duplexes and sidewalks and trees. Instead, Sofia could see enormous skyscrapers, glittering with glass and chrome against a dazzling blue sky. The scooter stood on a street that seemed older than the fancy buildings a few blocks away. Here, the buildings were short and squat, with a worn, friendly feeling. Each apartment had a small balcony, where potted plants spilled leafy vines down the walls. It all felt oddly familiar, though Sofia knew without a doubt that she'd never been here before.

But . . . was it possible she had *seen* it?

"Papai's photo," she whispered. One of Papai's most treasured belongings was a family photo taken outside his home in Brazil. It was a color photo of his relatives in São Paulo, including the cousins that Sofia hoped to meet someday. The more

she thought about the photo, the more Sofia was convinced that her relatives had been standing on this very street. And if she was right . . .

Sofia turned to Sam. "I know this is going to sound crazy," she said, "but I think we're in Brazil!"

"What?! Are . . . are you kidding?" Sam said. "How did we get to *Brazil*?"

Sofia quickly told Sam about Papai's missing

scrapbook. "He can't remember if he left it back at the apartment where he grew up," she said. "So when the scooter asked where we wanted to travel, this is where I told it to go. And now, here we are!"

"Are you sure?" Sam asked.

Sofia told him about the family photo. "This is where it was taken," she said.

"But *how*?" Sam asked, trying to puzzle it out. "Brazil is thousands of miles from Compass Court! Unless Aunt Charlie . . . "

"The scooter!" Sofia said. She hopped off the seat and Sam stood back too.

Sam shook his head. "I knew Aunt Charlie was working on something big," he said. "But this is huge! This could change the world! If people could really travel anywhere in the world in an instant—"

"*Shhh!*" Sofia held a finger to her lips. A figure had appeared in the doorway of the nearest

apartment building, and Sofia had a funny feeling that they should keep Aunt Charlie's latest invention top secret, at least for now.

The person in the doorway looked at Sam and Sofia. When he stepped out of the shadows, Sofia noticed that he was a boy about her age. And that wasn't all they had in common. They shared the same curious smile and their noses looked almost exactly the same. They were even about the same height. They stood there, staring at each other, for a long moment. They stared so hard that neither one of them noticed the **click-click** of Sam's camera.

"Lucas?" Sofia finally asked.

"Sofia?" the boy asked. "Is that *you*?"

4
The Scooter Secret

Sofia turned to Sam, who was still taking dozens of photos. **Click-click! Click-click!** "Sam, this is my cousin, Lucas," she said, beaming. "Lucas, this is my best friend, Sam."

Sam poked his head out from behind the camera. "I had a feeling this was going to be a moment to remember," he said with a grin. "Say cheese!"

Sofia threw her arm around Lucas's shoulders and grinned at the camera. "Cheeseburger!" she joked.

Click-click!

"What are you doing here?" Lucas asked, still shocked. "Where are your parents? I didn't know you were coming to visit."

"Neither did I," Sofia said. She turned to Sam. "Should we tell him?"

"I think we have to," Sam said, and Sofia nodded. She quickly told Lucas all about Aunt Charlie's latest invention and their astonishing journey to São Paulo.

"That's incredible!" Lucas said. He moved closer to the red scooter for a better look. "And it will take you anywhere in the world?"

Sam and Sofia exchanged a glance. "Yeah—at least, we think it will," Sam said. "This is our first time testing it out."

"How did the scooter know to bring you here?" asked Lucas.

"Well," Sofia began, "a little while ago, I was helping Papai look for his scrapbook. He can't find it anywhere and he started to wonder if he left it in one of the hiding places in his old bedroom. So when the scooter asked where we wanted to go, I thought of Brazil right away. I never thought it would actually work!"

Lucas's eyes widened. "Your papai's old room is *my* room now," he said. "And it has lots of great hiding places!"

Sam looked at Sofia, who grinned in return.

She turned to Lucas. "Do you mind if we take a look?"

"Are you kidding? A special invention brought you across the world. Let's find that scrapbook!"

Lucas said. "Follow me."

Sam and Sofia wheeled the red scooter into a narrow passageway between two buildings. In the shadows, it was hardly noticeable, and the friends wanted to keep it that way—especially since the scooter was their ride back to Compass Court, and they had to get back to the community center to help set up for the potluck dinner.

With the scooter tucked away, they clambered through the entryway of the building and followed Lucas into the apartment.

Halfway up the stairs, though, Sofia suddenly stopped. She could hear a woman singing in Portuguese. "Is that my Tia Beatriz?" she whispered.

Lucas nodded. "Mamãe always sings when she's cooking," he said.

"Whatever she's making smells delicious," Sam said.

"Come on! Mamãe and Papai will be so excited to meet you," Lucas said. "They'll probably throw a big party tonight!"

Sofia's heart buzzed at the thought of a São Paulo family party, but something made her hesitate. She slumped against the stairwell. "I . . . I really want to meet them, too," she said. "But how will we explain everything? They'll call my parents, and they'll be upset that I'm so far away, and what would happen to the scooter?"

Sam looked worried, too. "Would they be

mad at Aunt Charlie?"

"Would Aunt Charlie be mad at us?" Sofia asked.

Lucas glanced up toward the doorway and nodded. "I understand," he said. "We'll go straight to my room. Mamãe will never even know you're here."

Lucas, Sofia, and Sam crept down the hall to Lucas's bedroom. The walls were covered with posters of famous soccer players ("It's called *futebol* here," Lucas told them), and a shelf next to Lucas's bed was crowded with cool seashells. Red curtains fluttered in the gentle breeze coming through the open window.

"Wow," Sofia said. "I can't believe this was Papai's bedroom when he was a kid! I wonder what it looked like back then."

"Check this out," Lucas said. He showed Sofia the frame around the closet, where several notches had been carved into the wood. "This is where our grandparents marked your papai's height each year!"

"Amazing," Sofia breathed, touching each notch with her fingertip.

Sam leaned over to snap a picture. "Say cheese," he said.

Sofia posed next to the notches on the doorframe. "Cheese and crackers!" she said.

Click-click!

"Now, you said the scrapbook was in a hiding place?" Lucas asked.

"Yes," Sofia said. "But Papai couldn't remember the place."

"Well..." Lucas said thoughtfully. "There's a half shelf in the back of the closet that you can't see unless you stand on a chair."

Lucas dragged his desk chair over to the closet and perched on top of it. He patted and poked at the shelf, then shook his head. "No scrapbook here," he said. "Just some cobwebs."

"Hey, while you're up there, what about the ceiling?" Sam asked.

"Yes!" Sofia said. "That's where Papai was looking back at the community center, under the ceiling tiles."

All three looked up. There were no tiles or trapdoors that could be moved aside to reveal something hidden—just a smooth, flat ceiling.

"Oh well," Sofia said with a sigh. "It was a good idea."

Everyone was silent for a moment as they tried to figure out where to look next.

"Papai was looking up," Sofia said slowly. "But what about . . . down?"

"Down?" Sam repeated.

Sofia nodded. "If the scrapbook isn't behind a

ceiling tile, could it be under a floorboard?"

Lucas gasped. "Over here!" he said.

Lucas ran across the room to the corner, where a knothole made an opening between two floorboards. "I lost my favorite marble down this hole when I was a little kid," he said. "I tried to fish it out, but I never thought to check the floorboard. I wonder . . ."

Lucas tried to hook his finger into the knothole, but it didn't fit. Next, he tried to use a pencil to pry one of the boards up from the side.

It didn't move.

"Sorry," he said. "It just won't budge."

"Wait a minute," Sofia said, digging in her pocket. She held up her chain of paper clips in triumph. "Let's see if this does the trick."

Sofia unbent the paper clips into skinny wires, then twisted them together to form a strong hook. She fished the wire hook into the hole and pulled until she felt it catch under the board. Then all three of them pulled back on the hook and—

Pop!

5
The Hiding Place

The floorboard came up so suddenly that Sofia tumbled backward into Sam and Lucas. They giggled as they steadied themselves.

Sofia held up the floorboard. "You were right, Lucas."

"I can't believe this hiding spot's been here all along," he said.

Sofia leaned closer to the gaping hole in the floor. "Pretty dark down here," she said over her shoulder to the boys, but before they could answer, she plunged her hand into the hole.

"Uh, Sofia?" Sam said. "There could be, like, spiders down there—"

"I like spiders," Sofia said, reaching deeper under the floorboards. The space under the floor was cool and smooth, but as Sofia moved her fingers, she could feel powdery dust coating them.

Other than that, the space was empty. Sofia's face scrunched up in a frown. She'd been so sure that Papai's scrapbook was hidden somewhere in his old bedroom.

She wasn't quite ready to give up, though. Sofia reached deeper and deeper, until her entire arm was under the floor.

"Sofia..." Sam said again.

"Just...a little...farther..."

Then, she felt it: Her fingertips grazed something smooth and hard. Something rectangular. Something with rough, papery edges.

Her eyes widened.

"Sam! Lucas!" she cried. "I think..."

With just the tips of her fingers, Sofia nudged the object closer and closer, until at last she could grab it. She steadied herself and carefully lifted her arm from the hole in the floor.

Her discovery was covered in a thick layer of dust, but they could all tell exactly what it was: an old book with a brown leather cover and yellowed pages. Sofia knew what it was even before she opened it.

"Papai's scrapbook!" she breathed.

"It's been here all along," Lucas said.

"And that's not all I found," Sofia said. She lifted her hand to reveal a small marble pinched between her fingers.

"My lucky marble!" Lucas said. He hugged his cousin and put the marble on the shelf next to his seashells.

Sam **click-clicked** a picture of the scrapbook. "What are you waiting for?" he asked. "Open it!"

Sofia took a deep breath and blew the dust off the cover. She ran her hand along the edge, but just as she was about to open it—

Knock-knock-knock!

6
An Unexpected Breeze

The three friends froze. Another knock rattled the door, and a woman's voice called, "Lucas?"

"That's Mamãe," Lucas whispered. "Quick!"

Sam and Sofia ducked behind the bed as Lucas

slid the floorboard over the hole and scrambled to the door. "*Sim, Mamãe?*" he said.

"*Está com fome?*" she asked in Portuguese. "*Eu fiz pão de queijo.*"

"She asked Lucas if he's hungry because she made some *pão de queijo*," Sofia translated for Sam in a whisper.

Lucas peeked around the bed. "I'll be right back," he said quietly. "And I'll bring you some of Mamãe's cheesy bread balls!"

"Thanks," Sam whispered back as Lucas slipped out of the room and closed the door behind him.

Sofia exhaled in a long, shuddery sigh. "That was close," she whispered.

"Yeah," Sam agreed as he leaned against the side of the bed.

Sofia looked down at the scrapbook. "I don't think I can wait for Lucas to open it," she said. "You think he'll mind?" Her fingers were practically twitching with anticipation.

"I don't think so," Sam said. "After all, it belongs to *your* dad."

"Okay," Sofia said. "Let's do it!" She lifted the cover and slowly began to turn the pages. There were ticket stubs from soccer games at Estádio Cícero Pompeu de Toledo, a program from a concert at the Sala São Paulo, and lots of drawings and photographs.

Sam nodded at the photos with appreciation. "Wow, check out Papai Luiz's pictures," he said. "They're so good!"

"Papai almost became a photographer before he started drawing and painting," Sofia said. When she turned the page, her breath stuck in her throat.

"Look!" she said.

Sofia held up a card that had been pressed between the pages of the scrapbook. It was old and stained. The writing on it, in spindly cursive,

was in Portuguese. Sofia couldn't understand all the words, but she recognized the words on the front right away. It read "*Mousse de Maracujá.*"

"My great-grandmother wrote this," Sofia said in wonder. She turned to Sam. "Look—it's her top secret recipe, the one Papai was looking for!"

Sam and Sofia jumped as the bedroom door swung open again—but it was only Lucas. He was carrying a big carton of *água de coco* and a plate piled high with *pão de queijo*.

Whoosh!

The opening of the door created a gust of

wind that lifted the recipe card out of Sofia's hand. It fluttered into the air—and right out the open window!

7
Special Delivery

"**N**o!" Sofia cried as she dashed over to the window. But it was too late. The recipe card was gone.

"I can't believe it," Sofia groaned. "We came all this way! I had it in my hands. Can you see it? Where'd it—"

"There!" Sam said. He pointed out the window. "Check out the top of that truck. Is that it?"

Sofia squinted. A huge grin crossed her face as she spotted it. The yellowed card had come to rest on the top of a delivery truck that was parked at the curb.

"Sam! You found it!" she exclaimed.

"Hurry," Lucas urged them. "That truck delivers food to the *mercadinho* all the time. It's the little store on the corner. We'll run down and get the recipe before the truck leaves for its next delivery."

Sofia scooped up Papai's scrapbook and the three friends ran out of Lucas's room and hurried quietly down the stairs.

Out on the street, they stared up at the truck. It seemed even bigger now that they were on the ground.

"Don't worry," Sam said, as if reading Sofia's mind. "I can get it."

Sam jumped onto the truck's back bumper, where a narrow metal ladder led to the roof. He climbed up easily and pulled himself onto the top of the truck, where he disappeared from view.

"Sam?" Sofia called out. "You okay up there?"

A few moments later, Sam's face appeared at the top of the truck. He grinned in triumph as he held up the recipe. "Got it!" he announced.

"Yes!" Sofia said, shooting her arms in the air. "Now come down before—"

At that moment, they heard it: the unmistakable sound of the truck's engine rumbling to life. A look of alarm crossed Sam's face. He shoved the recipe card deep into his pocket and disappeared from view.

"Sam!" Sofia called.

"Hurry!" Lucas cried.

But it was too late. The truck had already pulled away from the curb, with Sam still on top!

"Follow that truck!" Sofia cried.

8
The Chase

"How do we follow it?" Lucas asked. "It's already halfway down the street!"

"Come with me," Sofia said.

She led Lucas to the parked scooter, slid the scrapbook into the secret compartment beneath the seat, pulled out two black helmets, and hopped on with her cousin. In seconds, a familiar message flashed onto the screen.

Sofia paused. She didn't know where, exactly, the delivery truck was heading, so she didn't know what to type. She stared at the control panel, deep in thought, until she noticed a small button below the screen.

"Yes! Of course!" Sofia exclaimed. "This *is* a scooter, after all. We can just . . . drive it!" She pushed the button, then said over her shoulder to Lucas, "Hang on!"

"Do you know how to drive this thing?" he asked.

"We're about to find out."

She twisted the handle, and there was a loud **scrrreech!**

Sofia carefully steered the red scooter onto the road and past the apartment buildings. Then they lurched forward and zipped into traffic. Up ahead, she could see the delivery truck. She twisted the handle to speed up, and with the wind whipping through her hair, she felt like she was speeding down a racetrack.

"Where do you think the truck will go next?" Sofia called back to Lucas.

"I have no idea," he replied. "It could make deliveries anywhere in the city or country!"

"That's what I'm worried about," Sofia said. "Hold on tight, Sam! We're coming for you!"

But up ahead, she could see that Sam wasn't holding on tight—at least, not as tightly as he should have. He was sitting up on the truck now, gripping the edge with one hand and snapping photos with the other. Even over the wind, she could hear the familiar sound. **Click-click! Click-click!**

"That's so Sam," Sofia said, grinning as she shook her head.

"It's pretty brave to take pictures from the top of a moving truck," Lucas said, impressed.

They passed an enormous stadium and Sofia heard the **click-clicking** once again.

"Papai always says that Sam has a great eye,"

Sofia said. "He must be using it now. I bet those pictures will be amazing, even if he doesn't know exactly what he's looking at."

As if in response, the scooter's touch screen lit up and started pointing out each landmark that they passed. The stadium was called Estádio Cícero Pompeu de Toledo. Sofia remembered the ticket in Papai's scrapbook and smiled. **Click-click!** A short while

later, they rode by Ibirapuera Park, which was filled with bicycle paths, museums, and even a planetarium. **Click-click!**

As Sam snapped photos, Sofia steered the scooter through the streets, doing her best to stay close behind the truck. After some twists and turns, she found herself gazing up at a large building made of beige stone. It had graceful, arching windows filled with panes of glass that glittered in the sunlight. Two beautiful domes were perched high above the entrances. From where Sofia sat on the scooter, the building looked like it took up an entire city block!

"Wow," Sofia breathed. "What's *that*?"

"Oh, that's the Mercadão," Lucas told her, and sure enough, the scooter's screen flashed the words Mercadão Municipal de São Paulo.

"It's an enormous marketplace," Lucas said as they rode by. "You can get almost any food in the world there! There are these giant columns inside that go all the way to the ceiling, and stained glass windows that show where all kinds of food come from."

Sofia gasped. "Look!" she cried as she spotted a vendor carrying a crate of passion fruit into the market. "Passion fruit! That's just what Papai needs for his passion fruit mousse. I wish we could go in and buy some."

"You might get your wish," Lucas said. He let

go of her shoulders to point at the delivery truck ahead.

The truck had stopped moving and Sofia pulled up right behind it. They were at a red light, which gave Sam the perfect opportunity to get down.

"Sam! Sam!" Sofia cried. "Red light! Climb down! Hurry!"

9
Out of Town

Sam, who was focused on photographing the Mercadão, snapped to attention. "Right! Coming!" he said. His head moved back and forth as he glanced between the traffic light and the ladder at the back of the truck.

"Don't worry, we'll watch the light," Sofia called to him. "Quick, get down before it changes to green!"

"I'm coming!" Sam yelled back. He clambered across the back of the truck. Just as he reached the ladder, though, Sam gasped.

"What's wrong?" Sofia called, still watching the light.

"My camera!" Sam yelled back. "It's stuck!"

From the scooter, Sofia could just see the camera's strap snagged on a sharp metal bolt on the roof of the truck. Sam tried to unhook the strap, but it wouldn't budge.

"The light's going to change any second," Lucas said, worried.

"Sam's fast," Sofia said. "I'm sure he'll be—"

"Got it!" Sam exclaimed, holding his camera up in triumph.

"We'll celebrate later. Get down quick before the light changes and the truck starts moving again!" Sofia urged him.

Sam was just about to climb down the ladder when suddenly—

The red light flashed to green and the truck lurched forward.

"GREEN!" Sofia and Lucas screamed.

Sam instantly pressed himself flat on top of the truck, holding on as it ambled toward the Mercadão.

"Maybe it's going to stop to make a delivery here," Sofia said hopefully.

Unfortunately, the truck kept driving right past the market. Even worse, it seemed to be picking up speed.

"Sofia?" Lucas said slowly. There was a note of worry in his voice that she noticed right away.

"Uh-oh," she said. "What's wrong?"

"I think . . . " Lucas said. "I think the truck is leaving São Paulo!"

10
An Unbelievable Beach

Sure enough, the truck rumbled through downtown São Paulo and onto a highway that led out of the city. It didn't look like there would be any more traffic lights for quite a while. As their adventure grew even more unpredictable, Sofia knew there were about a hundred different things she could worry about. But Sam, who was still **click-clicking** his camera from the top of the truck, didn't seem concerned. And as the red scooter zoomed down the highway, Sofia couldn't help but feel a thrill of anticipation sparkle in her heart.

Where would their unexpected adventure lead them next?

The tall skyscrapers of downtown São Paulo fell behind them as they drove toward shorter buildings like the one where Lucas and his family lived. The highway curved through towns and then fields, before the delivery truck and red scooter crossed a bridge over a body of deep blue water and continued onto a long strip of land.

They were now traveling through such mountainous areas that Sofia couldn't see any buildings at all. "Where on earth is this truck taking us?" she wondered.

"I guess we'll find out soon enough," Lucas replied.

For more than an hour, the truck and the scooter continued their journey. The crisp scent of saltwater on the air made Sofia's nose twitch. Eventually, they drove into another busy city with many buildings and vehicles: cars and trucks and even boats in the harbor. And that was where the truck finally shuddered to a stop.

Sofia and Lucas jumped off the red scooter and hurried over to the delivery truck. They stood ready to help Sam as he descended the metal ladder at last.

"Wow, what a ride!" he exclaimed. "Where are we?"

"We're in a city called Santos," Lucas replied. "It's a seaport, and unless I'm wrong . . . "

Lucas's voice trailed off as he hurried away from the road, down a path, and through a garden dotted with trees. Sofia turned back to Sam. He seemed a little unsteady on his feet, so Sofia reached out and held onto his arm.

"Are you okay?" she asked.

Sam nodded. "My legs are kind of wobbly. Whoa!"

"What now?" Sofia asked.

Sam started laughing. "My hair!" he said as he raised his hand to his head. "You didn't tell me my hair was standing up all crazy!"

Sofia laughed, too. "Wobbly legs and wild hair seem like a small price to pay for what must have been the best and most unique tour of São Paulo in the history of the world," she told him. "I can't wait to see your pictures!"

"Good," Sam said, grinning. "Because I took a ton of them!"

"And I have great news, too," Sofia added. "The scooter mapped our route, so we have lots of info on all the amazing landmarks we passed."

"That's awesome," Sam said. "We'll have to work on a scrapbook of our own! With my pictures and your words . . . "

"We're going to have a pretty amazing story to tell when we get home," Sofia said. Then her smile faded a little.

"Home," she repeated. "I almost forgot."

"Me too," Sam said. "That was such an incredible ride, it was hard to think of anything else."

"We have to go back soon for the Compass Community Center potluck dinner," Sofia said with a sigh. "I wish we could stay in Brazil longer."

"I wish we could stay forever," Sam said.

Just then, Lucas appeared at the end of the path. "Sofia! Sam! You've got to see this!" he yelled.

Sofia and Sam knew they had to go home soon, but surely they had enough time to see what Lucas was so excited about.

They ran toward Lucas and followed him down the garden path. "Welcome to the beach," he said, throwing his arms out wide. "I *knew* I'd been here before! Mamãe took me here last year to watch the boats come in to port."

For a moment, Sofia was completely speechless. Good thing a picture is worth a thousand words. That familiar sound— **Click-click! Click-click!**—told

Sofia that Sam was already taking dozens of pictures beside her.

The sparkling ocean stretched out to the horizon and beyond. It was a brilliant shade of blue, somehow even deeper and brighter than the cloudless sky overhead. The air was filled with the sound of waves lapping on the shore and gulls cawing as they soared through the sky. They could see several massive cruise ships in the distance, each as big as a floating city.

Sofia didn't even stop to think. She kicked off her shoes and wiggled her toes in the soft white sand. Then, laughing with glee, she ran down to the ocean and skipped through the seafoam. Sam and Lucas were right behind her.

After several minutes of splashing through the surf, the friends clambered back onto the dry sand. Sofia tried to catch her breath.

"That was amazing," she said. "If you'd told me that we'd be splashing in the waves in Santos

when I woke up this morning—"

"You never would have believed it," Sam finished for her.

"And I never would've believed that my American cousin and her best friend would show up for a surprise visit," Lucas added.

"You know what?" Sofia said. "I'm glad that

Papai accidentally left his scrapbook back in São Paulo! And I'm even glad that the oven broke and Aunt Charlie had to go fix it. Otherwise, we might not have had this adventure. And it's been incredible."

"Papai Luiz will be so happy when we bring him the long-lost recipe," Sam chimed in. "I can't wait to taste the *mousse de maracujá*."

"Me too," Sofia replied. Then a wistful look crossed her face as she looked out at the ocean. "I just wish we could've brought Papai some of that fresh passion fruit we saw at the Mercadão," she added. "He always says the passion fruits we buy at home are never quite as good as the ones he remembers from when he was a boy."

"Well, if you want really fresh passion fruits . . ." Lucas began. "I mean, *really, really* fresh passion fruits . . ."

Sofia and Sam turned to face him. He smiled knowingly back at them.

"We could always go pick some ourselves," he said.

"But how?" Sofia asked.

Lucas gestured toward the red scooter. "If it can bring you all the way from Compass Court to São Paulo, I bet it can take us into the Amazon rainforest," he replied.

11
The Amazing Amazon

"**L**ucas!" Sofia cried. "That's an amazing idea." Then she turned to Sam. "What do you think? Do we have time for a quick detour?"

Sam checked his watch with a worried look

on his face. "What time does the potluck start again?" he asked.

"Six o'clock," Sofia replied. "But if we hurry..."

"The rainforest can be really dangerous, though," Sam added. "It has poisonous frogs, deadly anacondas, vicious piranhas..."

Then, to Sofia's surprise, a grin spread across Sam's face. "Let's do it!" he said. "Who knows when we'll get the chance to visit the Amazon again?"

"To the red scooter!" Lucas announced.

"One second," Sofia said, holding up a finger. She didn't want to leave this beautiful beach without a special souvenir to help her remember this moment. In her pocket, Sofia found the almost-empty tin of jelly beans. She shared the candy with the boys, then scooped up some of the soft sand and added a small seashell on top. Sofia knew she would treasure these tiny mementos forever.

Then Sofia, Sam, and Lucas returned to the red scooter, brushed the sand from their clothes, and climbed on board. The same yellow letters flashed across the screen, asking them where they'd like to travel. This time, Sofia knew exactly what to type.

Whiz ...

Zoom ...

FOOP!

Sofia realized that she and Sam could have done a better job preparing Lucas for the dazzling power of the scooter. One minute they were in the bright sunshine, listening to the sound of the ocean. The next thing they knew, the scooter flashed and rumbled, and the warm, humid air of the Amazon rainforest was pressing in on them as chirps and chatters of wild animals filled their ears.

Lucas stumbled off the scooter. "Did we . . . are we . . . is this . . . ?" he asked.

"Yup!" Sofia replied as she helped her cousin steady himself. "Pretty cool, huh?"

"That might be the understatement of the year," Lucas said. "It happened so fast! *How?*"

"You'd have to ask my Aunt Charlie," Sam said.

"I still can't believe it myself," Sofia said, giggling.

The three of them took in the sights of the

rainforest. The thick canopy of trees and vines overhead blocked out much of the sunlight, but once their eyes adjusted to the dim light, Sofia, Sam, and Lucas could see incredible wonders of nature all around them: Ancient trees with deep grooves in the bark. **Click-click!** A dew-speckled spiderweb nearly as tall as Sam. **Click-click!** A sleepy, furry sloth dozing as it hung from a tree. **Click-click!**

With his camera, Sam captured it all.

"We've studied the Amazon in school," Lucas told Sam and Sofia. "It has thousands of different types of animals. Howler monkeys. Jaguars! And there are more than a thousand different types of birds. My favorite's the toucan. But maybe the coolest thing about the rainforest is that there are tons of plants and animals here that haven't even been discovered yet."

"The Amazon is amazing," Sofia said. She rummaged in her pocket for her little notebook and scribbled a new item on her ever-growing to-do list.

Lucas looked up into the canopy of leaves and branches overhead. "Passion fruits grow on vines," he explained. "In the rainforest, they have to grow pretty high. They have long green leaves, feathery-looking flowers, and are a yellowish color."

Sam and Sofia looked up, too. The three friends were quiet as they searched for a passion fruit vine.

Suddenly, Sam reached into his messenger bag. "I have an idea," he said. He pulled out a second camera with a long lens.

"He has all kinds of cameras," Sofia explained to Lucas.

Whirrr!

Sam twisted the barrel of the camera to extend the zoom lens and pointed it at the tree canopy. There was silence as he scanned the greenery, searching for a vine that fit Lucas's description.

"Through this, all the leaves look huge, like parts of an emerald city," Sam said.

"See any passion fruit?" Sofia asked.

"Not yet..." Sam peered back and forth, then stopped, twisting the zoom further. "But I see a vine! It's twined around an old tree with a wide trunk and thick branches. Lucas, is that a passion fruit vine?"

Lucas peeked through the camera's viewfinder. "Yes! You found one!" he said.

The three adventurers grinned. They knew

what to do next: start climbing! The grooves in the tree's trunk made it easier to climb than they expected. They scaled the tree, hand over hand, foot by foot, until at last they reached the vine. It drooped under the weight of plump passion fruits. The fruits were so ripe that they seemed to fall into Sofia's outstretched hand as soon as she touched them. Soon, Sam's messenger bag was full to the brim.

"Do you think that's enough?" Sam asked, staring at the bulging bag.

"I sure hope so!" Sofia said. She laughed as

she struggled to close it. "We'll be eating passion fruit for *days*."

"Sounds good to me," Sam said, licking his lips. "I'm getting really hungry."

"Me too," Sofia said.

"Me three," Lucas added. "It must be getting close to dinnertime."

They climbed back down to the forest floor.

"So, where should we go now?" Lucas asked.

Sam and Sofia exchanged a glance. Neither one of them wanted to say the words, but they knew they had no choice.

"Home, I guess." Sofia sighed. It had been such an incredible adventure that she didn't want it to end. "We have to get the recipe back for a big potluck at the community center."

Sam glanced up at the canopy of green overhead. "You can't see the sun down here, but you can still tell it's getting dark," he said. "I always know it's time to head home when it gets too dark to take photos."

"Yeah," Lucas said, his voice tinged with sadness. "My parents will probably start wondering where I am."

"Selfie time!" Sam said suddenly. He and Sofia squeezed in on either side of Lucas against a backdrop of broad leaves and bright flowers. All three of them grinned at the camera.

"Say cheese," Sam said.

"Cheese fries!" Sofia exclaimed.

Click-click!

"Perfect," Sam said.

Then the three friends boarded the red scooter once more.

Sofia's face was illuminated by the glowing screen as she typed in Lucas's address.

Whiz . . . Zoom . . . FOOP!

12
One Last Stop

In an instant, the red scooter transported everyone back to São Paulo. The streetlights were starting to flicker on, but none were as bright as the glittering flash made by the red scooter as it arrived back in front of Lucas's apartment building.

"I guess we have to say goodbye now," Lucas said slowly as they stepped off the scooter.

Sofia tilted her head to one side. "I'm not so sure about that," she replied. "I have a funny feeling that we're going to see each other again. Maybe sooner than we even know."

"I hope so," Lucas replied. Then he turned to Sam. "Would you send me a copy of our rainforest selfie?"

"Of course," Sam told him.

And that gave Sofia an idea.

"Pen pals!" she exclaimed. "We can be pen pals and write letters back and forth all the time!"

"Let's do it," Lucas agreed. "I want to know where the scooter will take you next!"

"Well, our next stop will be Compass Court," Sofia replied. "But after that . . . who knows?"

Sam climbed back onto the scooter behind her.

"Goodbye, Lucas!" Sam and Sofia called out together. Sofia's fingers slid across the screen as she typed *COMPASS COURT*. "Good—"

Whiz . . . Zoom . . .

"—bye!"

. . . FOOP!

13
No Place Like Home

Sofia blinked and, just like that, they were back in Aunt Charlie's garage. On the counter, Aunt Charlie's computer was in the process of calculating a long, complicated equation. Beakers and flasks gleamed in the late-afternoon sunlight. Nothing had changed since they left. It was later in the day, but everything else was exactly the same.

Well, not exactly *everything*. Sofia and Sam were different now. Their adventures in Brazil, from São Paulo to Santos to the Amazon rainforest, had changed them forever.

Sam plugged the scooter into its charger as Sofia retrieved Papai's scrapbook from the compartment beneath the seat.

"I think we made it back just in time," Sam said.

"Come on," Sofia said. "Let's find Papai. He's going to be so surprised!"

Sam and Sofia raced back to the community center. They found Papai in the dining room arranging some long tables. Sofia held the scrapbook behind her back.

"*Olá*, you two," Papai said. "Where've you been? The potluck starts in an hour!"

Sofia opened her mouth, then closed it.

"Ahh, say no more," Papai said with a knowing smile. "Let me guess. Charlie's working on something top secret?"

Sam and Sofia exchanged a look.

"You could say that," Sam said.

"Sam and I have a surprise for you," Sofia said.

"A few surprises, actually," Sam added. He reached into his pocket and pulled out the creased recipe card as Sofia held out the scrapbook.

The look of astonishment on Papai's face was something that Sofia would never forget. "But . . . is that . . . my scrapbook?" he gasped. "And this . . . this is my *avó's* recipe! How on earth—where did you find this?"

"Let's just say it was where you would least expect it," Sofia said mysteriously.

"You're full of secrets and surprises today," Papai said staring down at the card. "Thank you. I had just about given up hope that I would ever see this recipe again. Come, let's go to the store and see if they have any ripe passion fruit."

"*That's* where our last surprise comes in," Sofia said. She gestured to Sam's messenger bag. "Ta-da!"

When Sam opened the bag, Papai's eyes grew wider than ever. "Sofia! Sam! These *maracujás* are just like the ones I remember from home!" he exclaimed. Papai leaned closer to the passion fruit and inhaled deeply. "Ahhh, that delicious smell. I'd know it anywhere."

He gave Sofia and Sam a big hug. "I don't

know how you did this, but thank you," he said. "How exciting to share my *avó's mousse de maracujá* with everyone at the potluck!"

"I can't wait to try it!" Sofia said.

"Come, let's go to the kitchen," Papai announced. "I'll teach you both how to make *mousse de maracujá.*"

When they arrived at the kitchen, Aunt Charlie was packing up her toolbox. "The oven shouldn't give you any more trouble, Lyla," she was telling Sofia's mom.

"Thank you, Charlie," Mama replied. "You've saved my famous extra cheesy lasagna!"

"Lyla, look," Papai said. "Perfectly ripe passion fruit! Now I can make *mousse de maracujá* to share with everyone tonight."

"Wonderful! Just as long as you don't need that oven," Mama joked. "It's taken!"

"We only need the fridge and some expert kitchen assistants," Papai said.

"I'm sorry I was gone for so long," Aunt Charlie told Sam and Sofia. "How's the red scooter?"

Sofia and Sam stared at each other. What should they say? Where to begin? But before either one of them could speak, Aunt Charlie grabbed one of the passion fruits and smiled.

"I thought it maybe still needed a few adjustments," she said, "but it looks like it's working just fine."

And then, Sofia could hardly believe her eyes, but she thought she saw Aunt Charlie *wink* at them.

Sofia sneaked a glance at Sam. He was looking at her, too. In that moment, she knew that they were both thinking the exact same thing: The red scooter was better than fine. It was incredible.

"Come on, kids," Papai urged them. "The *mousse de maracujá* isn't going to make itself!"

A short time later, the tart, creamy passion fruit mousse was chilling in the fridge when the first neighbors started arriving for the potluck.

The Wassermans brought noodle kugel. Mrs. Ling made a platter of dumplings.

There were fried plantains and spicy curry and crunchy falafel. Couscous, tamales, sushi, quiche—soon Papai had to get an extra table just to hold all the delicious dishes that everyone had brought to share.

The community center's dining room was filled to the brim with friends and neighbors, and Sofia's heart was filled to the brim, too. She could tell from the smile on Sam's face that he felt the same way.

"Remember when I said that I wished we could stay in Brazil forever?" he asked. "Brazil is amazing, but I changed my mind. There's no place like home."

"There's no place like home," Sofia agreed, nodding her head. "But you know what?"

"What?" Sam asked.

"Brazil feels a little bit like home to me now, too," she said.

Someone else might not have understood what Sofia meant, but Sam was her best friend for a reason. A knowing smile crossed his face as he pulled something out of his pocket.

"I know what you mean," he told her, handing her a small photo. "This is for you. I printed it in

Papai Luiz's office."

It was the picture of the moment when Sofia and Lucas had first met. She knew she would treasure the photograph almost as much as the memory. "Thanks, Sam!" she whispered.

"There's a whole world out there," Sam said.

Sofia held the photo close and felt that familiar sparkle in her heart.

"Just imagine," she said, "where else the scooter might take us."

Fim
(The End)

Portuguese Terms

- Água de coco – Coconut water

- Avó – Grandma

- Brasil – Brazil

- Fim – The end

- Futebol – Soccer

- Mamãe – Mom

- Mercadinho – Small market

- Olá – Hello

- Pão de queijo – Cheese bread

- Papai – Dad

- Mousse de maracujá – Passion fruit mousse

- Vamos! – Let's go!

Portuguese Phrases

- Está com fome? – Are you hungry?

- Sim, Mamãe? – Yes, Mom?

- Olá, minha filha! – Hello, my daughter!

- Eu fiz pão de queijo. – I made cheese bread.

- Diário do Luiz – Luiz's Diary

Sofia and Sam's Snippets

São Paulo is the largest city in Brazil. It's an industrial town, filled with buildings of different shapes and styles. It is located on a plateau on the coast, near the Atlantic Ocean.

Brazil is home to the largest Portuguese-speaking population in the world. Brazilian people are known for their energetic spirits, their commitment to family, and their rich musical and culinary culture.

Brazil is the largest country in South America. It borders every other country on the continent except Ecuador and Chile.

The Amazon River flows through northern Brazil, providing water to the jungles and rainforests that surround it. The Amazon is not a single river, but actually a series of smaller rivers and waterways.

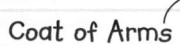
Coat of Arms

National Flag

The national flag of Brazil is green and gold, with a blue orb in the center with a white band. The color gold symbolizes wealth, the color green represents the country's nature, the color blue represents the sky and Brazil's rivers, and the white band symbolizes peace.

Futebol (soccer) is the national sport of Brazil. The national team has won the World Cup finals five times, which is more wins than any other country.

Coffee is one of Brazil's main agricultural exports. In fact, Brazil produces more coffee than any other country in the world. Some of the ships that set sail from the port city of Santos transport coffee across the world.

Brazil is home to the largest variety of animals of any country on earth. Hundreds of mammal species, thousands of fish and bird species, and an estimated 100,000 insect species live in Brazil's rainforests, swamps, and semidesert regions.

National Bird:
Sabiá-Laranjeira or
Rufous-Bellied Thrush

Animals of the Amazon

- [ ] Toco toucan
- [ ] Anteater
- [ ] Three-toed sloth
- [ ] Piranha
- [ ] Capybara
- [ ] Caiman
- [ ] Anaconda
- [ ] Jaguar
- [ ] Poison dart frog
- [ ] Howler monkey
- [ ] Spider monkey
- [ ] Scarlet macaw
- [ ] Amazon river dolphin

Papai Luiz's Family Recipe: Mousse de Maracujá

Ingredients:

- [ ] 6-8 passion fruits
- [ ] 1 can (14 oz) sweetened condensed milk
- [ ] 3 cups heavy cream
- [ ] Garnish (see suggestions below)

Details:

Active Time: 30 minutes
Total Time: 1 hour 30 minutes
Yield: 6 servings

Mousse de Maracujá

Instructions:

1. Cut the passion fruits in half and empty the seed-filled pulp into a bowl with a spoon. If needed, you can use a small amount of water to rinse extra juice from the skins of the fruit.

2. Break up the pulp with your hands for about a minute to release as much juice as possible.

3. Use a fine strainer or food-safe cloth to strain the juice from the pulp.

4. Add the sweetened condensed milk to the juice and stir the mixture together.

5. Use an electric hand mixer to beat the cream until it becomes fluffy and whipped. You can also use a whisk to beat the cream by hand. Stiff peaks should hold their shape on the mixer or whisk when lifted from the cream.

6. Little by little, fold the whipped cream into the passion fruit mixture. Stir slowly and gently so the ingredients are blended without the cream losing its airy texture.

7. Spoon the mousse into individual bowls or glasses and chill in the fridge for at least an hour.

8. Once chilled, top with your favorite garnish and enjoy!

Suggested Garnishes:

- [ ] Fresh passion fruit
- [ ] Mint
- [ ] Coconut shavings
- [ ] Roasted nuts
- [ ] Chocolate shavings
- [ ] Cocoa powder

Keep your adventure going with a World Edition subscription!

Explore the world one country at a time.

Ages 6-10

Dive into world exploration and discover exciting countries and cultures. Loaded with hands-on projects, activities, and souvenirs, you'll have everything you need for a jet-setting adventure!

LittlePassports.com